Jacques and de Beanstalk

by Mike Artell

illustrated by Jim Harris

DIAL BOOKS FOR YOUNG READERS

an imprint of Penguin Group (USA) Inc.

For Sesina Paige Marshall with love from her Papa Mike

DIAL BOOKS FOR YOUNG READERS • An imprint of Penguin Group (USA) Inc. • Published by The Penguin Group
Penguin Group (USA) Inc., 375 Hudson Street, New York, NY 10014, U.S.A. • Penguin Group (Canada), 90 Eglinton Avenue East, Suite 700, Toronto, Ontario, Canada M4P 2Y3
(a division of Pearson Penguin Canada Inc.) • Penguin Books Ltd, 80 Strand, London WC2R 0RL, England • Penguin Ireland, 25 St. Stephen's Green, Dublin 2, Ireland (a division
of Penguin Books Ltd) • Penguin Group (Australia), 250 Camberwell Road, Camberwell, Victoria 3124, Australia (a division of Pearson Australia Group Pty Ltd) • Penguin Books
India Pvt Ltd, 11 Community Centre, Panchsheel Park, New Delhi - 110 017, India Penguin Group (NZ), 67 Apollo Drive, Rosedale, North Shore 0632, New Zealand (a division of
Pearson New Zealand Ltd) Penguin Books (South Africa) (Pty) Ltd, 24 Sturdee Avenue, Rosebank, Johannesburg 2196, South Africa • Penguin Books Ltd, Registered Offices:
80 Strand, London WC2R 0RL, England

Text set in Granjon • Manufactured in China on acid-free paper

3 5 7 9 10 8 6 4 2

Library of Congress Cataloging-in-Publication Data
Artell, Mike.
Jacques and de beanstalk / by Mike Artell; illustrated by Jim Harris.   p. cm.
Summary: In this Cajun version of "Jack and the Beanstalk," a handful of magic beans takes Jacques up through the clouds to the castle of a hungry giant.
ISBN 978-0-8037-2816-5
[1. Stories in rhyme. 2. Fairy tales. 3. Giants—Folklore. 4. Folklore—England.] I. Harris, Jim, date, ill. II. Jack and the beanstalk. English. III. Title.
PZ8.3.A685Jac 2010 398.2'094202—dc22 [E] 2009005188

The full-color artwork was prepared using watercolor and pencil on Arches watercolor paper.

GLOSSARY

ALLONS—pronounced "al-ON," it is French for "Go!"

BAYOU—pronounced "BY-you," it is a small river or stream.

CAYENNE—pronounced "KI-an," it is a hot red pepper.

CHER—pronounced "share" (the R is very soft), it is a term of affection meaning "dear."

COURTBOULLION—pronounced "KOO-be-yawn," it is a fish stew made with herbs, spices, and tomatoes.

MAIS—pronounced "may," it is used to add excitement or emotion to the words that follow.

MON AMI—pronounced "mawn ah-ME," it is French for "my friend."

MON DIEU—pronounced "mawn DEW," it is French for "my goodness."

POULARDE—pronounced "POO-lard," it is the French word for "hen."

TOUTE DE SUITE—pronounced "toot SWEET," it is French for "right away" or "quickly."

SUGGESTIONS FOR READING THIS STORY ALOUD

This story has been written to be read aloud. Each line of the rhyming verse consists of eleven beats. In order to get the best results, the reader should emphasize the second, fifth, eighth, and eleventh beats in each line.

For example, the first two lines of this story are:

    If you like dem stories, I got one fo' you

    about a young boy who live down de bayou.

When reading aloud, put extra emphasis on these syllables:

    If YOU like dem STOries, I GOT one for YOU

    aBOUT a young BOY who live DOWN de baYOU.

ADDITIONAL NOTE: The word "MaMA" in this story should be read with an emphasis on the second syllable. The unusual capitalization of the third and fourth letters of the word reflects that pronunciation.

If you like dem stories, I got one fo' you
About a young boy who live down de bayou.
Dey call dis boy Jacques and he live in a house
Wit' his old MaMA and a little brown mouse.

Now Jacques and MaMA, dey sho' po', dat's fo' true
And sometime dey worry what dey gon' do.
Dey ain't got no rice and dey ain't got no bean,
Dere shelves dey all empty like you never seen.

Dey know dey need food, and dey need dat food NOW
An' so dey decided to sell dere ol' cow.
Jacques tie up dat cow wit' a rope he done found,
Den walk down de road dat lead right into town.

When Jacques get to town, he go put up a sign
Dat say, "Cow fo' sale, ya'll. Now don't she look fine?"
De people pass by and dey say, "Whoo she is nice!
If dat cow was twins, you could sell dat cow twice!"

But one man walk by, den he stop and walk back.
He say, "Mais! Dat cow sho' is fine . . . dat's a fack!
Now, how much you t'ink that cow's worth, mon ami?"
And Jacques smile and say, "I don' know . . . you tell me."

Dat man lean waaay back, and he squint both his eye,
He pooch out his lips and he make a big sigh.
He walk roun' dat cow wit' his arms folded tight,
Den say, "I t'ink five magic beans is 'bout right."

Jacques twis' up his finger inside of his ear,
'Cause he don' believe what he t'ink he done hear.
"Five magic beans!? You must t'ink dat you fonny.
  Dem beans may be magic, but I need some money!"

De man say to Jacques, "You could live like a king.
Wit' five magic beans you can have anyt'ing.
Don' pass up dis chance, 'cause it may be your last.
If you want dese beans den you got to act fast."

So Jacques he t'ink hard about what he should do,
He know dat dem beans sound too good to be true.
But he trade his cow for dem beans dat man got.
An' Jacques say, "MaMA gonna t'ank me a lot."

But dat's not exactly what happened dat day.
When Jacques tol' MaMA, cher, she don' say, "Hoo-ray!"
Instead she done act like she gon' pass out.
Her face turn all red and den she start to shout.

"You went to de town wit' a cow and come back
Wit' nothin' but five little beans in a sack?
Now what ever made you believe dat ol' man?
Mais, all we got now is dem beans in yo' han'."

She snatch up dem beans, den she squeeze 'em real hard,
She tro' 'em outside and dey land in de yard.
She turn roun' to Jacques and she make a big frown.
"Now go to your room until I can cool down."

De next day when Jacques go and look out de door,
His eyes dey see somethin' dey don't see before.
Out front in de yard there ain't no place to walk
And dat's 'cause de whole yard be fulla beanstalk.

Dat beanstalk is bigger aroun' den a tree
De top is so high dat it's too tall to see.
"I KNEW dat dem beans had some magic!" Jacques shout.
"Dey grew in our yard when MaMA t'roo dem out.

"I bet if I climb pass de clouds to de top
I'll find out exactly where dis beanstalk stop."
Jacques grab him a branch and den he start to climb
He get to de top, but it take a long time.

Jacques find dat de tip of dat beanstalk done lay
In front of a castle dat's big, tall, and gray.
De door of dat castle be twenty feet tall.
He can't get it open 'cause Jacques he's too small.

Jacques knock on de door and it don't take too long
De door swing wide open, but dere's somet'in' wrong.
De lady who answer de door look real mean.
She don' look like nuttin' dat Jacques ever seen.

But den she see Jacques, and she say, "Ain't dat cute?
Dis boy by my door ain't as big as my boot."
And soon a big smile come all over her face.
"I made courtboullion. Maybe you'd like a taste?"

Den Jacques say, "Merci, dat is my favorite dish.
I LOVE courtboullion when it got dat redfish."
Dat lady give Jacques all de food he can eat
And Jacques he so hungry, he eat it tout de suite.

Den jus' as he finish an' take de las' bite,
Jacques hear somet'in' loud an' it give him a fright.
De sound make his hair stand up straight on his head.
De sound was de voice of a man, and it said:

"I smell me some cayenne when I sniff de air,
So dat means a Cajun's aroun' here somewhere.
It's time fo' my lonch an' I t'ink I'll have some
When I find dat Cajun ya'll, fee fi fo fum."

"Mon Dieu!" say de lady. "De giant come back.
You better go hide fo' you end up his snack!"
Jacques jump in de bread box an' quick close de door,
An' in walk de giant and he say once more:

"I smell me some cayenne when I sniff de air,
So dat means a Cajun's aroun' here somewhere.
It's time fo' my lonch an' I t'ink I'll have some
When I find dat Cajun ya'll, fee fi fo fum."

De giant he sniff and he make his face frown.
"Now, where is dat Cajun? I know he's aroun'!"
De lady shout back, "What you talkin' about?
Dere's nobody here. Don't you make all dat shout.

"De cayenne you smell is what I sprinkled on
De redfish when I made dis nice courtbouillon.
Now, sit youself down and I'll fix you a plate.
Dis might be de best lunch dat you ever ate."

De giant sat down and he eat all dat food,
But dat still don't help him get in a good mood.
He push back his plate, den he stand on his legs
And he roar, "Where's my chicken dat lay golden eggs?"

Jacques t'ink to himself, "Golden eggs? Dat's for true?
Dat's somethin' most chickens don' know how to do.
A chicken like dat would be somethin' to see.
And whew! T'ink how rich dat ol' giant must be."

Jacques slip out de bread box and crawl on de floor
And watch as de giant walk out de back door.
He hear from de yard lotsa cackles and squawks,
And soon dat ol' giant come back wit' a box.

Inside of dat box Jacques could see on de straw
De skinniest chicken dat he ever saw.
Jacques t'ink to himself, "Now, I know dis ain't right.
Dat chicken look like it done been up all night."

"Allons!" shout de giant. "I'm waitin' on you.
I want me some eggs made o' gold, dat's fo' true!
Now lay me an egg!" shout dat giant real rough,
De chicken start shakin' and she start to puff . . .

Dat bird close her eyes and when she try her best,
She lay one small egg of pure gold in dat nest.
But layin' dat egg wear dat chicken plumb out.
When she fall asleep, dat ol' giant he shout:

"Wake up, you dumb bird. You got more work to do.
You laid me one egg, but I gotta have two."
But it was no use; dat bird can't lay no more,
De giant get mad and he storm out de door.

Jacques climb on de table and say to de hen,
"Wake up, Madame Poularde, he'll be back again.
If you want to go, I will take you wit' me.
You can stay wit' de giant or you can be free."

"I want to be free," say de chicken, "for true.
I ain't stayin' here, boy, I'm going wit' you."
Dey climb off de table and jump on de floor,
Jus' when dat ol' giant walk back troo' de door.

"What's dis?" say de giant. "I knew I was right!"
I see me dat Cajun right dere in plain sight.
I need some dessert and I t'ink you'll do fine.
You run if you want, but you gonna be mine!"

"Pardon Monsieur giant," Jacques say wit' a smile,
"You couldn't catch me if we ran for a mile."
And den just to make dat ol' giant get mad,
Jacques stick out his tongue (but don't do dat . . . it's bad).

GOLDEN CHICK

Around and around dat big castle dey ran;
 De chicken and Jacques and de big giant man.
'Til finally, dey ran out de door and dey found
 De place where de beanstalk done lay on de ground.

Den Jacques and de chicken slide down that big vine
And land on de ground by MaMA's ol' clothesline.
Before dat ol' giant could start to slide down
Jacques chop down de vine and it fall to de ground.

And things sho' were different fo' everyone den.
'Cause Jacques let MaMA have dat magical hen.
MaMA treat dat hen like it's her favorite pet.
Dat hen lay more eggs than she ever did yet.

I don' know fo' sure if dat story is true,
But down where de Cajuns live on de bayou,
When dey tell dem stories, dey shore like to talk
About dat boy Jacques and his magic beanstalk.